A CHRISTMAS STORY

BRIAN WILDSMITH

Oxford University Press

A long time ago in the town of Nazareth,

a little donkey was born.

When the donkey was almost nine months old, his mother had to go on a long journey with her mistress and master, Mary and Joseph.

Mary and Joseph asked Rebecca, who lived nearby, to look after the little donkey while they were away.

The little donkey was sad without his mother
and he wouldn't eat.

So Rebecca said to the little donkey that
they would go to look for his mother.
And they set out to follow Mary and Joseph.

'Have you seen a man and a woman
with a donkey?' Rebecca asked a traveller.

'Yes, they passed me on the road to
Jerusalem,' he said.

Soon Rebecca and the little donkey met a
soldier standing guard at a splendid palace.
'Have you seen a man and a woman

with a donkey?' Rebecca asked.
'Yes, they passed this way,' said the soldier.
'Now hurry along. King Herod is busy.'

After a time, they met some shepherds watching over their flocks. 'Have you seen a man and a woman and a donkey?' Rebecca asked.

'Yes, they were going towards Bethlehem,'
replied the shepherds.

And so Rebecca and the little donkey went on.
Then suddenly they heard glorious music,

and they saw a great star shining down
on the little town of Bethlehem.

When they reached Bethlehem, they met a man
standing in the doorway of an inn. Rebecca asked
if he had seen Mary, Joseph, and the donkey.

'Yes,' he replied. 'They wanted to stay here,
but there was no room at the inn. They went
to the stable over there.'

The stable was bathed in a wonderful light
that shone from the bright star above.

As Rebecca and the little donkey came near,
they heard the sounds of a mother donkey
braying and a little baby crying.

Rebecca and the little donkey entered the
stable. And there, lying in a manger, was
a new-born baby.

'What are you going to call him?' asked Rebecca.
'His name is Jesus,' said Mary.

In the days that followed the little donkey and
his mother went with Mary and Joseph and

the baby Jesus into Egypt. And Rebecca rode
home on a king's camel.

And it came to pass that Mary and Joseph returned to Nazareth, and there Jesus grew up, with Rebecca as his friend.

FOR LITTLE ORNELLA

Oxford University Press, Walton Street, Oxford OX2 6DP

Oxford is a trade mark of Oxford University Press

First Published 1989 Reprinted 1989, 1990
First published in paperback 1991
First published in miniature 1992
Reprinted 1992

Hardback ISBN 0 19 279872 3   Paperback ISBN 0 19 272244 1
Miniature ISBN 0 19 279947 9

British Library Cataloguing in Publication Data
Wildsmith, Brian
A Christmas Story
I. Title
823' .914[J]

Printed in Hong Kong